NO FLEAS, PLEASE!

Written by Michael J. Pellowski
Illustrated by John Jones

Troll Associates

Library of Congress Cataloging in Publication Data

Pellowski, Michael
  No fleas, please!

  Summary: All of the animals try to get rid of the
flea when it lands on them.
  [1. Fleas—Fiction. 2. Animals—Fiction]
I. Jones, John, 1935-   ill.   II. Title.
PZ7.P3656No   1986   [E]   85-14066
ISBN 0-8167-0608-5 (lib. bdg.)
ISBN 0-8167-0609-3 (pbk.)

NO FLEAS, PLEASE!

Boing! What is that sound?
Boing! Boing! It is the sound of
a flea jumping. Boing! Boing!
Boing!

A flea was jumping through the woods. He jumped by a big lake. He jumped by big trees. What was that silly flea doing?

The flea was looking for a place
to live.

Where is a good place for a flea to live? A lake is not a good place. A tree is not a good place. A good place is on an animal.

Fleas like to live on animals. But animals do not like fleas. Fleas make animals itch. Fleas make animals scratch.

Boing! Boing! The flea jumped
and jumped. He looked and
looked for an animal to live on.

Big Bear was an animal. He
lived in the woods. The flea saw
Big Bear.
"There is a good place to live,"
thought the flea. Boing!

"What was that sound?" said
Big Bear.
He could not see the flea. But he
could feel the flea. What a bad
feeling it was!

12

"Oh no," cried Big Bear, "not a flea! Please, not a flea!"
But a flea it was. And Big Bear began to feel itchy. Poor, itchy Big Bear!

Big Bear scratched. He
scratched the itch. He scratched
here, there, and everywhere. Big
Bear scratched at the flea. But
the itching did not stop.

14

"This flea must go," yelled Big
Bear. "I must find a better way
to scratch!"
Big Bear had a scratching tree.
Bears like to scratch their backs
on trees. Big Bear's tree was by
the lake. He went to scratch his
big itch.

"Now I will make this flea go away," said Big Bear. He scratched his back on the tree. Up he went. Down he went. Up and down he went scratching, scratching, scratching.

Nosey Otter was in the lake. He
saw Big Bear. Otters are very
nosey.
"What is that silly bear doing?"
said the otter. "I will go and
see."

Nosey Otter went up to Big Bear.
"Why are you scratching?"
Nosey Otter asked.
"I have a big itch," said Big
Bear. "A flea is on me."

"A flea," yelled the otter. "No fleas, please!"

Poor Nosey Otter. Being too
nosey was bad for him. The flea
saw the otter.

"A bear is not a good place to
live," thought the flea. "Bears
scratch too much. An otter is a
better place to live."

Boing! What a sound! What a happy sound for Big Bear. What an unhappy sound for Nosey Otter.

"I feel better," said Big Bear.
"I do not feel itchy anymore."
Instead Nosey Otter felt an itch.
He had the flea.

Big Bear went away. Nosey
Otter scratched and scratched.
Oh, what a bad feeling! Poor,
poor, itchy Otter.

"This flea must go," cried Nosey
Otter.
Down to the lake went the
otter. Into the lake he jumped.
The flea held his nose.

24

Up and down went Nosey Otter
in the lake. He came out. He
did not feel better. The itching
did not stop. Nosey Otter
scratched and scratched.

Raccoon was by the lake.
Raccoons like to live by lakes.
He saw Nosey Otter scratching.
Up to Nosey Otter went
Raccoon.
"You look silly," he said.

"I am not silly," said Nosey
Otter. "I am itchy. A flea is on me."
"A flea," cried Raccoon. "No
fleas, please!"

The flea saw Raccoon.
"An otter is not a good place to
live," thought the flea. "Otters
go in lakes. I do not like lakes.
A raccoon is a better place to
live."

Boing! Nosey Otter stopped
scratching—what a happy
feeling! Raccoon began to itch—
what an unhappy feeling! Poor,
itchy Raccoon!

Into the lake jumped Nosey Otter. Away he went. Through the woods went Raccoon. Scratch! Scratch! Scratch!

"A flea! Why me?" cried
Raccoon. "This flea must go.
This itching must stop!"

Up a tree went Raccoon.
Raccoons like to go up in trees.
Up, up, up he went. He
scratched and scratched and
scratched.

In the tree was Busy Squirrel.
He was going down the tree.
Busy Squirrel saw Raccoon
scratching. He stopped being
busy.
"What are you doing?" he said.

"I have an itch," said Raccoon.
"I am scratching."

34

Raccoon's flea had a bad feeling. It did not like being up, up, up a tree.
"A raccoon is not a good place to live," thought the flea. "A squirrel is a better place. This squirrel is going down the tree."

Boing! Raccoon felt better. The
itch was gone.
"What was that sound?" said
the squirrel.
Raccoon cried, "It was the flea!"

"A flea," yelled Busy Squirrel.
"No fleas, please!"
Down the tree went Busy
Squirrel. Down went the flea.

Busy Squirrel began to itch. But he was too busy to scratch. Back up the tree he went. Down the tree he went. Up! Down! Up and down—what a busy, busy squirrel.

Busy Squirrel stopped.
"This flea must go," said
Squirrel. "I cannot be busy and
itchy, too."
He began to scratch and scratch.

Busy Squirrel sniffed. He smelled something. Busy Squirrel stopped scratching. "It is Smelly Skunk," he cried.

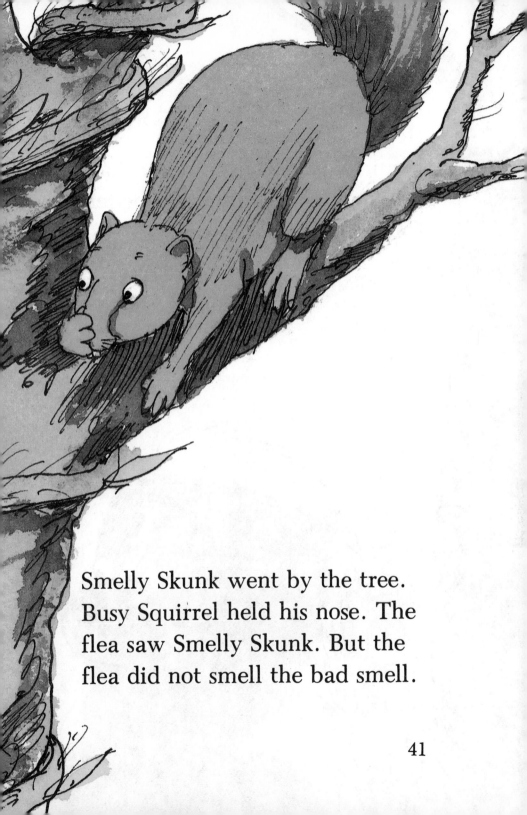

Smelly Skunk went by the tree.
Busy Squirrel held his nose. The
flea saw Smelly Skunk. But the
flea did not smell the bad smell.

"A squirrel is not a good place to live," thought the flea. "A squirrel is too busy. There is an animal. That animal is a better place to live."

Boing! What a happy sound for
Busy Squirrel. The itching
stopped. Up the tree he went.

Smelly Skunk stopped. He began
to feel itchy. He scratched and
scratched. Poor Smelly Skunk.

The poor flea—*now* he smelled
the skunk. What a bad smell! It
smelled here. It smelled there. It
smelled everywhere!

"This animal is not a good place to live," thought the flea. "This animal has a bad smell!" Boing! Off the skunk jumped the flea.

Boing! Boing! Boing! Through
the woods the flea jumped. He
was looking for a place to live.
A bear was not a good place.
An otter was not a good place.
A raccoon was not a good place.
A squirrel was not a good place.
And a skunk was not a good
place.

Where is a good place for a flea
to live? Not by me! No fleas,
please!